FOX ON WHEELS

by Edward Marshall
pictures by James Marshall

PUFFIN BOOKS

For Darrell Hill

PUFFIN BOOKS
Published by the Penguin Group
Penguin Books USA Inc., 375 Hudson Street, New York, New York 10014, U.S.A.
Penguin Books Ltd, 27 Wrights Lane, London W8 5TZ, England
Penguin Books Australia Ltd, Ringwood, Victoria, Australia
Penguin Books Canada Ltd, 10 Alcorn Avenue, Toronto, Ontario, Canada M4V 3B2
Penguin Books (N.Z.) Ltd, 182–190 Wairau Road, Auckland 10, New Zealand

Penguin Books Ltd, Registered Offices: Harmondsworth, Middlesex, England

First published in the United States of America by Dial Books for Young Readers, 1983
Published in a Puffin Easy-to-Read edition, 1993

5 7 9 10 8 6 4

LIBRARY OF CONGRESS CATALOGING-IN-PUBLICATION DATA
Marshall, Edward.
Fox on wheels / by Edward Marshall;
pictures by James Marshall.   p.   cm.—(Puffin easy-to-read)
"Reading level 1.9"—T.p. verso.
"First published in the United States of America by Dial Books
for Young Readers, a division of Penguin Books USA Inc., 1983"—T.p. verso.
Summary: Fox babysits for his sister Louise, learns to climb a tree
for some grapes, and wins a shopping cart race.
ISBN 0-14-036541-9
[1. Foxes—Fiction.]
I. Marshall, James, 1942– ill. II. Title. III. Series.
[PZ7.M35655Fq 1993]
[E]—dc20   93-2722   CIP   AC

Puffin® and Easy-to-Read® are registered trademarks of Penguin Books USA Inc.
Printed in the United States of America

Reading Level 1.9

DOCTOR
FOX

On Saturday
Carmen called Fox
on the phone.
"Dexter and I are going out
on our skateboards," she said.
"I'll be right over,"
said Fox.

"Not so fast, Fox," said Mom.

"I'm taking the twins to the doctor.
And you must stay with Louise."

"Rats!" said Fox.

"Now, none of that," said Mom.

Fox told his friends

that he could not go out.

"And all because of *you*,"

he said to Louise.

"Now, don't give me any trouble."

Soon Fox was lost

in his TV programs.

He did not give Louise

another thought.

All of a sudden

there was a loud crash.

It came from the backyard.

"Uh-oh," said Fox.

Louise had taken a bad spill.

"Oh my gosh!" cried Fox.

"Louise is dead!"

But Louise was not dead.

"Help!" said a tiny voice.

"Get me out of here!"

Fox was very upset.

"It's all my fault," he said.

"It's all my fault!"

"I want to go to my room,"
said Louise.

"Of course," said Fox.

"I want to lie down," said Louise.

"Of course," said Fox.

"I need soft music," said Louise.

"Of course," said Fox.

"Make a tuna sandwich," said Louise.

"Of course," said Fox.

"Read me a story," said Louise.

"I'll be glad to," said Fox.

"Are you feeling better?" said Fox.

"Not much," said Louise.

"What can I do now?" said Fox.

"Rub my toes," said Louise.

"Certainly," said Fox.

"Mmmm," said Louise.

Just then Louise's friends
Spud and Dora Jean came by.
"Can Louise come out?" they said.
"I'm afraid not," said Fox.
"Louise has had a bad spill."

"Just a minute," said Louise.

And she hopped right out of bed.

"I'm much better now," she said.

And she ran outside to play.

"Hmmm," said Fox.

FOX AND
THE GRAPES

One day Fox was riding his bike

in the park.

"Gosh," he said.

"This makes me really hungry."

Just then, something fell

out of a tall tree.

It was a grape.

"That's odd," said Fox.

"Grapes don't grow on trees."

"Hi," said a voice.

Fox looked up

and saw Millie.

She was eating

a bunch of grapes.

"I love grapes," said Fox.

"Want some?" said Millie.

"Yes, please," said Fox.

"Come on up," said Millie.

"Uh," said Fox.

Fox didn't like high places.

Not one little bit.

"Just drop some down,"

he said.

"Oh, no," said Millie.

"You have to come up."

"Uh," said Fox.

"You aren't afraid, are you?"

said Millie.

"Of course not!" said Fox.

"Then climb up,"
said Millie.

"All right," said Fox.

"Here I come."

Fox took a deep breath.

He closed his eyes.

And he started

to climb the tall tree.

But he made a serious mistake.

He opened his eyes

and he looked down.

"Oooh," he said.

"I'm so high up!"

And he climbed back down.

"What's the matter?"

said Millie.

"Nothing," said Fox.

"I'll be right up."

He tried again.

But he came back down
this time too.

"I thought you weren't scared,"
said Millie.

"I'm not," said Fox.

"I just don't want
any grapes after all.
They're probably no good."

Fox went to another part

of the park

and sat down to think.

He was cross with himself.

He really *didn't* want

any grapes now.

But he just *had* to climb that tree!

This time he got a running start.

And this time

he made it all the way

to the top.

"Oh, I'm so glad you're here,"

said Millie.

"I'm scared!

I don't know how to get

down!"

"Well, that's just *dandy*!"
said Fox.

"Want a grape?"
said Millie.

FOX
ON
WHEELS

One Saturday morning

Fox ate breakfast in a hurry.

"I'm off to meet the gang!" he said.

"Hold your horses," said Mom.

"But we're going to have

a bike race!" said Fox.

"You can race later," said Mom.

"I need some help around here."

"Doing what?" said Fox.

"Take your choice," said Mom.

"You can look after Louise.

Or you can go shopping."

Fox looked at Louise.

"Too much trouble," he said.

"I'll shop."

"Here is the list," said Mom.

"This will take *all day*!" said Fox.

"Then you must hurry," said Mom.
"And don't forget the tuna fish
for Louise's sandwich."

At the market

Fox ran into the gang.

They had to shop too.

"We'll just have to race later,"

said Fox.

"Too bad," said Dexter.

"I have an idea," said Carmen.

"Why don't we race right now?"

"Great idea!" said her friends.

"Let's race from one end of the store

to the other!" said Fox.

"Fine!" said the gang.

41

"On your mark, get set, go!"

cried Fox.

And the race was on!

Dexter pulled out ahead.

"Gangway!" he cried.

Suddenly a wheel fell off his cart.

"Nuts!" said Dexter.

"I'm out of the race!"

"Beep, beep!" cried Carmen.

And shoppers ran for their lives.

Carmen was about to win.

But just then her cart

crashed into a barrel of pickles.

"Oh, fudge!" said Carmen.

"Hooray!" cried Fox.

"I won, I won!"

But some of the shoppers
had angry words for Mr. Sloan.
"Shopping here is *dangerous*!"
said nice Mrs. O'Hara.

"It won't happen again,"
said Mr. Sloan.

When Fox got home,

his mom was on the phone.

"Oh, really?" said Mom.

"He didn't!

He *did*?

Well, it won't happen again!"

And she hung up.

"I hear you're the fastest

fox on wheels," said Mom.

"You bet I am," said Fox.

"Care to prove it?" said Mom.

"I'll get my bike," said Fox.

"Hold your horses," said Mom.

"I have a better idea."

"Rats!" said Fox.

"These aren't the wheels
I had in mind!"